A Note to Parents

We often consider humankind's sinfulness to be the main theme of this story because Adam and Eve disobeyed God's command. However, woven into the story is a bright thread of God's loving care for us, even when we disobey. We have made sure that this telling of the story focuses on God's caring acts, such as providing the garden and giving Adam and Eve clothing when they must leave the garden. We do not want to burden children at such a young age with the "sinfulness of all humankind."

You might point out that Adam and Eve had a choice of whether or not to eat the fruit, and that God loved them even though they made the wrong choice. The Bible does not specify exactly what the fruit looked like, therefore we have chosen to make it unlike any fruits that children will know.

Help your child imagine how lovely the garden might have been. You can then discuss how caring for the environment helps God make our world a lovelier place. You might also talk about how the earth produces better food and plant life when we take care of it.

— *Delia Halverson*

Delia Halverson is the consultant for *Family Time Bible Stories*. An interdenominational lecturer on religious education, she has written nine books, including *How Do Our Children Grow?*

Scripture sources: ***Genesis 2 and 3***

FAMILY TIME
BIBLE
STORIES

ADAM AND EVE

Retold by Mary Martin

Illustrated by Bryn Barnard

TIME LIFE Kids

ALEXANDRIA, VIRGINIA

God created heaven and earth and all the animals. Then God created a man and named the man Adam. God put Adam in a beautiful garden in a place called Eden. All different kinds of trees and flowers grew there. A sparkling river ran through the garden, bringing water to all the living things.

God said to Adam, "This is your home. It is sunny and warm. Its trees are filled with food. You can eat fruit from any tree, but do not eat the fruit from the tree that grows in the middle of the garden. For this is the tree of knowledge of good and evil."

Then God brought all the animals to Adam. God said, "Give each animal a name."

Adam looked carefully at each one and then he named it.

God did not want Adam to be alone, so God created a woman. She would be a companion for

Adam and live with him in the garden of Eden.
Adam named her Eve.

Adam and Eve lived happily in the garden. They swam in the river and played with the animals. They cared for the trees and flowers that grew there. They always had enough to eat. They ate fruits from all the different trees in the garden. But they did not eat fruit from the tree of knowledge.

Then one day, Eve saw a serpent in the tree of knowledge.

"Eat the fruit of this tree," the serpent said.

"But God told us not to," Eve said. "Surely, God knows what is best."

"Nothing will happen to you. The fruit of this tree will make you as wise as God," said the serpent. "You will know everything."

Eve listened to the words of the serpent. As she looked at the delicious fruit, she forgot the words of God.

She picked a fruit and ate it. Then she gave some to Adam. He ate it, too.

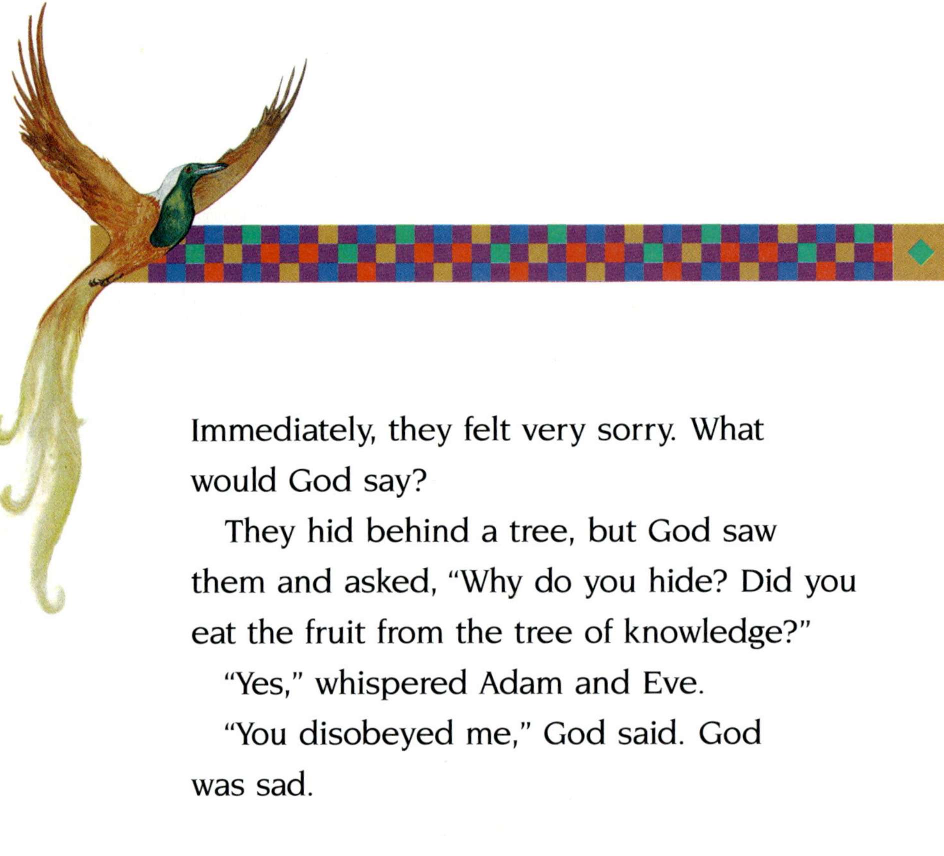

Immediately, they felt very sorry. What would God say?

They hid behind a tree, but God saw them and asked, "Why do you hide? Did you eat the fruit from the tree of knowledge?"

"Yes," whispered Adam and Eve.

"You disobeyed me," God said. God was sad.

Because Adam and Eve had eaten the fruit, they now knew the difference between good and evil. They knew the difference between right and wrong. They knew they had done wrong when they disobeyed God.

Then God said to Adam and Eve, "Because you disobeyed me, you must leave this beautiful garden."

Adam and Eve were very sorry and they cried as they left.

The world outside the garden of Eden was very different. It was not always sunny and warm. Because God loved them, God wanted to

protect Adam and Eve even though they had disobeyed. So God gave them clothes to keep them warm.

Adam and Eve made a new home in the land beyond the garden. They grew their own food. They worked hard and felt hunger and pain. But they felt joy, too.

They thanked God for all the good things in the world. They asked God for protection. And God continued to watch over Adam and Eve.

Time-Life Books is a division of Time-Life Inc.

TIME-LIFE INC.

PRESIDENT and CEO: George Artandi

TIME-LIFE BOOKS

PRESIDENT: John D. Hall
PUBLISHER/MANAGING EDITOR: Neil Kagan

FAMILY TIME BIBLE STORIES
ADAM AND EVE

Deputy Editor: Terrell D. Smith
Director, New Product Development: Elizabeth D. Ward
Marketing Director: Wendy A. Foster
Marketing Manager: Janine Wilkin
Editorial Assistant: Mary Saxton
Production Manager: Marlene Zack
Quality Assurance Manager: Miriam P. Newton

Produced by: Kirchoff/Wohlberg, Inc.
866 United Nations Plaza
New York, NY 10017

Series Director: Mary Jane Martin
Creative Director: Morris A. Kirchoff
Design and Production: Kelly T. Gabrysch
Jessica A. Kirchoff
David McCoy
Managing Editor: Nancy Pernick
Editor: Cynthia Rothman

First printing. Printed in U.S.A. Published simultaneously in Canada.

School and library distribution by Time-Life Education,
P.O. Box 85026, Richmond, VA 23285-5026.
TIME-LIFE is a trademark of Time Warner Inc. U.S.A.
For subscription information, call 1-800-621-7026.

Library of Congress Cataloging-in-Publication Data

Martin, Mary.
Adam and Eve / retold by Mary Martin; illustrated by Bryn Barnard.
p. cm — (Family time Bible stories) Summary: Retells the Biblical story of Adam and Eve, who lived happily in a beautiful garden until they disobeyed God.
ISBN 0-7835-4633-5
1. Eden—Juvenile literature. 2. Fall of man—Juvenile literature. 3. Forbidden fruit—Juvenile literature. 4. Bible stories, English—O.T. Genesis. [1. Adam (Biblical figure) 2. Eve (Biblical figure) 3. Bible stories—O.T.] I. Barnard, Bryn, ill. II. Title. III. Series.
BS1237.Q37 1996 96-15331
222'.1109505—dc20 CIP
AC